Humanity's End

Tyler Gornall

Published by Life Is A Disco Productions LTD,
2024.

HUMANITY'S END
First edition. October 12, 2024.

Written by Tyler Gornall.
Compiled/Edited by Rhys Jones.

Published by Life Is A Disco Productions LTD

Contents

Chapter 1
The Discovery

The late afternoon sun cast long shadows over the small, suburban neighbourhood of Brookside. It was the start of summer break, and the air was filled with the sounds of laughter, distant lawnmowers, and the occasional bark of a dog. The neighbourhoods' kids, freed from the constraints of school, were out in full force, their adventures only limited by their imaginations.

At the edge of Brookside, where the houses gave way to a dense forest, a group of four teenagers were deep in conversation. Mike, the tallest of the group with sandy blonde hair and an athletic build, was the natural leader. His sharp blue eyes sparkled with curiosity and a hint of mischief. Beside him, Jenny, a petite girl with curly red hair and a smattering of freckles across her nose, listened intently. She was known for her quick wit and adventurous spirit. Sam, a lanky boy with messy brown hair and glasses that often slipped down his nose, was the brains of the group. His thoughtful brown eyes were always analysing, always questioning. Lastly, there was Leah, a girl with long, straight black hair and an air of quiet confidence. Her dark eyes seemed to see right through to the heart of things, and her calm demeanour often balanced the group's more impulsive tendencies.

"C’mon, guys, I swear I saw somin’ fall in the woods," Mike insisted, his voice full of excitement. "It looked like a meteor or something, we gotta go check it out."

"You sure, Mike?" Jenny asked, her eyes wide with curiosity. "It could be dangerous."

"That's why we gotta go," Mike replied, already heading towards the tree line. "Besides, when have we ever backed down from a little danger?"

Sam adjusted his glasses and shrugs. "He's got a point; this could be a once-in-a-lifetime discovery."

Leah nodded; her expression thoughtful. "al'ight, but we need to be careful. We don't know what we're dealing with here."

The group moved swiftly through the forest, their excitement growing with each step. The trees soon began to thin, revealing a small clearing bathed in the orange glow of the setting sun. In the centre of the clearing was a small crater, and in the middle of that crater lay a smouldering meteorite, about the size of a beach ball. It glowed faintly, pulsating with an eerie, otherworldly light.

"Whoa," Mike breathed, stepping closer. "This is sick man."

Jenny crouched down; her eyes fixed on the meteorite. "Look at that," she said, pointing to a strange, shimmering substance oozing from a crack in the rock. "What is it?"

Sam pulled a small notebook from his backpack and began scribbling notes. "I've never seen anything like it," he muttered. "It could be some kind of extraterrestrial material."

Leah leaned in, her eyes narrowing as she studied the substance. "We should take a bit and analyse it," she suggested. "But we need to be really careful."

Mike nodded and carefully scooped a bit of the substance onto a stick. It was a deep, iridescent blue, and seemed to shimmer and shift as if alive. "What do you think it is?" he asked, holding the stick up for the others to see.

"No clue," Sam replied, his eyes wide with fascination. "But it doesn't look like nothing from Earth."

Jenny reached out and touched the substance with a finger. It was surprisingly cool to the touch, and she felt a strange tingle run up her arm. "This is so weird," she said, rubbing her fingers together. "It feels... alive."

The group sat in a circle around the meteorite, passing the stick with the strange substance between them. Each of them took a turn examining it, their minds racing with possibilities.

"Do you think it's edible?" Mike asked suddenly, a mischievous grin spreading across his face.

"Are you blinkin' crazy?" Leah exclaimed, though her eyes sparkled with intrigue. "We don't know what it could do to us."

"C'mon, it could be fun," Mike insisted. "Besides, if it is something dangerous, we need to know. Right, Sam?"

Sam hesitated, then nodded slowly. "I suppose, in the name of science, it wouldn't hurt to try a tiny bit. But we need to be cautious."

With a mix of excitement and trepidation, they each took a small dab of the substance on their fingers. One by one, they licked it, the taste strange and metallic. For a moment, nothing happened. Then, slowly, a warm, euphoric sensation began to spread through their bodies.

"Oh my god," Jenny giggled, her eyes wide and unfocused. "This is incredible."

Mike laughed, his usual composure slipping away. "I feel like I'm floating," he said, his voice dreamy.

Leah leaned back, her eyes closed, a peaceful smile on her face. "This is... amazing," she whispered.

Sam was the last to react, his analytical mind struggling to process the new sensations. But soon, even he was grinning, his thoughts a blur of colours and feelings.

For the next hour, the group lounged in the clearing, their senses heightened, their minds awash with strange, wonderful visions. They laughed and talked, their usual inhibitions falling away. It was an experience unlike anything they had ever known.

As the effects began to wear off, Mike sat up, his eyes bright with excitement. "We gotta share this with the others," he said. "This is too incredible to keep to ourselves."

Jenny nodded, still giggling. "Definitely, everyone needs to try this."

Leah and Sam exchanged a look, their earlier caution forgotten in the wake of their euphoric experience. "Okay," Leah said finally. "But we need to be careful, we don't want to attract too much attention."

The group gathered more of the strange substance, carefully storing it in a small jar Sam had in his backpack. As they made their way back to the neighbourhood, they felt a new bond between them, forged in the shared wonder of their discovery.

That night, they called their friends, inviting them to the clearing. One by one, their friends arrived, curious and excited. Mike, Jenny, Sam, and Leah shared the substance, explaining their earlier experience.

Before long, the clearing was filled with laughter and shouts of amazement as their friends experienced the same euphoria. It was a night of magic and wonder, a secret they all vowed to keep.

But as the sun rose, casting its first light over the sleepy town of Brookside, none of them could have foreseen the consequences of their discovery. What they had found was more than just a strange substance from a meteorite. It was something powerful, something unknown, and their lives were about to change in ways they could never have imagined.

Chapter 2
The Cravings

The morning after their incredible discovery, the group of teenagers awoke with a mix of lingering euphoria and an unsettling new sensation. It was as if their bodies were vibrating at a higher frequency, every nerve ending alive with a strange, insistent hunger.

Mike was the first to notice something was wrong. As he dragged himself out of bed, his muscles aching, he caught a glimpse of himself in the mirror. His usually bright blue eyes were dull, ringed with dark circles. His skin, once healthy and tan, had taken on a grayish pallor.

"What the hell?" he muttered, running a hand through his disheveled hair. His fingers brushed against his cheek, and he winced at the unexpected tenderness. Peering closer, he saw that his skin was starting to peel away, revealing raw, red flesh beneath.

Panic rising in his chest, Mike grabbed his phone and sent a frantic group text: Guys we gotta meet
sum weird is happening

Within an hour, the group had gathered at their usual spot in the forest clearing. The sight of his friends did nothing to ease Mike's fears. Jenny's once-vibrant red hair hung limp, her freckled face now ashen. Sam's glasses barely stayed perched on his nose, and Leah's dark eyes were shadowed with fatigue. All of them bore the same signs of decay:

peeling skin, sunken eyes, and a pervasive sense of unease.

"What’s happening to us?" Jenny whispered, her voice trembling.

"I don’t know," Sam replied, his voice strained. "But it’s clear this is connected to that shit we licked."

Leah paced back and forth, her anxiety palpable. "We need to figure this out. What if it gets worse?"

As the group deliberated, Mike's stomach growled loudly, echoing through the clearing. He clutched his abdomen, a sharp, gnawing hunger tearing at his insides.

"I'm actually so hungry," he groaned. "But it's not like normal hunger. It's... different."

The others nodded in agreement, their faces contorted with discomfort.

"We need food," Sam said, his voice desperate. "Maybe that'll help."

They returned to the neighborhood, scouring their kitchens for anything that might sate their hunger. But no matter what they ate—cereal, fruit, sandwiches—nothing seemed to fill the void.

Frustrated and desperate, the group reconvened at Mike's house, their collective hunger growing unbearable.

"This ain't working," Jenny said, her eyes wild. "I feel like I'm starving, but food isn't helping."

Mike's mind raced, trying to make sense of their situation. He glanced at Sam, who was staring at his younger brother, Timmy, playing in the yard. Suddenly, a horrifying thought struck him.

"Guys," he said slowly, his voice shaking. "What if... what if it's not normal food we need?"

The others turned to him, confusion etched on their faces.

"What do you mean by that?" Leah asked, her voice wary.

"I mean," Mike continued, swallowing hard, "i have this craving for...... people."

The silence that followed was deafening. The idea was too gross, too unthinkable. And yet, as they looked at one another, they could see the same realization dawning in each other's eyes.

"No," Jenny whispered, shaking her head. "That can't be it."

But as the minutes ticked by, the hunger grew more insistent, more painful. It was as if their very survival depended on satisfying this primal urge.

"I can't take it anymore," Sam said suddenly, his

eyes locked on Timmy. "I'm sorry, but I need to eat."

Before anyone could react, Sam lunged at his brother, sinking his teeth into the boy's arm. Timmy screamed, but the sound was quickly cut off as Sam tore into his flesh. The others watched in horror, their own cravings surging to the surface.

Jenny, Leah, and Mike found themselves unable to resist. They joined Sam, their minds screaming in protest even as their bodies moved on autopilot. The taste of blood and flesh was intoxicating, the hunger finally sated.

When they finally stopped, the realization of what they had done hit them like a tidal wave. Timmy lay motionless, his body a bloody mess. Sam, tears streaming down his face, backed away in horror.

"Oh my god," he sobbed. "What the fuck have we done?"

The others stared at the scene, their minds reeling. The hunger had subsided, but the consequences of their actions were all too real.

"We're monsters," Leah whispered, her voice hollow.

"No," Mike said firmly, though his eyes betrayed his own fear. "We didn't choose this. We need to figure out what’s happening to us and how to stop it."

In the days that followed, the group kept to themselves, avoiding their families and friends. They hid the evidence of their crime, burying Timmy's remains deep in the forest. But the hunger returned, relentless and insatiable. And with it came another disturbing discovery: they had stopped aging. Their bodies, despite the decay, seemed to be in a state of stasis, immune to the passage of time.

Desperation drove them to experiment further with the substance. They needed answers, and they needed to understand the full extent of what they had become. But each experiment only confirmed their worst fears: the substance was a drug, a powerful, alien drug that had transformed them into something inhuman.

They discovered that the effects of the substance could be transmitted through their bites. Those bitten would experience the same cravings, the same decay, the same twisted immortality. It was a curse, spreading like a virus.

As they grappled with their new reality, the group made a pact. They would stick together, support each other, and find a way to reverse the effects of the substance. But until then, they would have to navigate their monstrous cravings, the threat of discovery, and the haunting knowledge of what they had done.

Brookside remained blissfully unaware of the horrors unfolding within its borders. But for Mike, Jenny, Sam, and Leah, the nightmare was just beginning. The cravings were their constant
companions, a reminder of the terrible price they had paid for their discovery.

Chapter 3
Infection

The infection began as a slow, insidious spread.
In the weeks following their discovery, Mike, Jenny, Sam, and Leah struggled to keep their cravings and their monstrous transformation a secret. But secrets have a way of unravelling, especially when driven by an insatiable hunger.

It started in Brookside, their quiet suburban haven, where the initial bite victims unknowingly carried the infection beyond the borders of the forest. The cravings took hold quickly, transforming friends and neighbours into hollow shells of their former selves. The infection spread with terrifying speed, leaving the town a husk of its former self.

As the infection spread, so did the whispers of a new, potent drug. It was said to provide an unparalleled high, an escape from the mundane.

Unwitting users sought out this mysterious substance, only to find themselves ensnared in its deadly grasp. Reports of the infection spread like wildfire, drawing the attention of law enforcement and health officials. But by then, it was too late. The infection had taken root, and nothing could stop its relentless march.

Within a month, Brookside was overrun. The once lively streets were eerily silent, the only sounds the shuffling footsteps and occasional moans of the infected. Homes stood abandoned, their occupants either dead or transformed. Those who remained struggled to survive, hiding from the infected and scavenging for food.

The infection spread beyond Brookside, creeping into neighboring towns and cities. Each new victim became a vector, transmitting the substance through bites and close contact. Panic set in as reports of the strange new disease flooded the media. Governments around the world declared states of emergency, but containment proved impossible.

As the infection spread, society began to unravel. Quarantines and curfews were imposed, but fear and chaos reigned. People turned on each other, desperate to protect themselves and their loved ones. The infected, driven by their insatiable hunger, roamed the streets, preying on the living.

Hospitals were overrun with the sick and dying. Doctors and nurses worked tirelessly, but there was no cure, no treatment. The infected, their bodies rotting from the inside out, could not be saved. The once vibrant human race was becoming a horde of decaying, ravenous creatures.

Mike, Jenny, Sam, and Leah watched in horror as the infection they had unwittingly unleashed consumed the world. Their own transformations had stabilized; they no longer aged, and their decay had slowed to a near halt. But the guilt and horror of their actions weighed heavily on them.

"We did this," Jenny whispered one night as they huddled in a makeshift shelter. "We caused this."

"We didn’t know," Sam replied, though his voice was hollow. "We couldn’t have known."

"But we still have to fix it," Mike said, determination in his eyes. "We have to find a way to stop it."

They travelled across the country, searching for answers. Everywhere they went, they saw the same scenes of devastation. Towns and cities lay in ruins, overrun by the infected. The smell of decay hung heavy in the air, a constant reminder of the nightmare they had unleashed.

In Washington D.C., they found the remnants of the government struggling to maintain control. Scientists and researchers worked around the clock, desperately searching for a cure. Mike and his friends offered themselves as test subjects, hoping their unique condition might hold the key to stopping the infection.

The scientists discovered that the substance from the meteorite was unlike anything on Earth. It bonded with human DNA, altering it in ways they couldn't fully understand. It granted immortality, but at a terrible price. The infected were neither alive nor dead, trapped in a state of perpetual decay.

Despite their best efforts, the scientists could not find a cure. The infection had spread too far, too fast. Billions were now infected, their bodies rotting away even as their minds remained trapped in a haze of hunger and pain.

As the months turned into years, the world became a desolate wasteland. Nature began to reclaim the cities, vines and trees growing through the concrete and steel. The few remaining humans banded together in small, isolated communities, struggling to survive in a world overrun by the infected.

Mike, Jenny, Sam, and Leah continued their search for a solution, refusing to give up hope. They traveled from one end of the continent to the other, seeking out remnants of civilization, old laboratories, and any clue that might lead to a cure. But as time went on, their hope began to wane.

One day, as they trekked through the ruins of what had once been New York City, Leah stumbled upon an old, decrepit laboratory. Inside, they found notes and equipment left behind by a scientist who had been studying the meteorite substance. Among the notes was a single, tantalizing clue: a reference to another meteorite that had landed in a remote part of the world decades earlier.

"This might be it," Mike said, his eyes lighting up with renewed hope. "If we can find this other meteorite, maybe we can find a way to reverse the infection."

And so, with a new sense of purpose, the four friends set out on their final journey. They traveled across the globe, through the wastelands and the remnants of human civilization, guided by the hope that they might still save the world from the horror they had unleashed.

But as they ventured into the unknown, they couldn't shake the feeling that they were racing against time. The infection had transformed every living creature on Earth, turning the planet into a living nightmare. And as they moved deeper into the heart of darkness, they wondered if redemption was still possible—or if they were
doomed to wander the earth, immortal witnesses to Humanity's End.

Chapter 4
The Astronauts' Arrival

In the vast emptiness of space, the deep hum of the spacecraft's engines was a comforting constant for the crew aboard the ESS Discovery. This state-of-the-art vessel, designed for long-duration space travel, had carried its crew on a mission of exploration and discovery to the far reaches of the galaxy. Onboard were six astronauts: Aria, Steven, Finn, Eve, Eliot, and Alex. Each was a specialist in their field, chosen for their expertise and resilience.

Aria, the mission commander, was a seasoned astronaut with short, jet-black hair and piercing green eyes. Her calm demeanor and quick thinking had seen the crew through numerous challenges. Beside her was Steven, the navigator, whose sandy hair and easygoing nature belied his meticulous attention to detail. Finn, the ship's engineer, was a towering figure with a broad build, his hands always busy with the intricate workings of the spacecraft. Eve, the biologist, had a quiet intensity about her, her dark hair pulled back in a neat ponytail as she cataloged the alien specimens they had encountered. Eliot, the medic, was a calming presence, his gentle eyes and soft-spoken manner putting everyone at ease. Finally, Alex, the communications specialist, was the youngest of the crew, his enthusiasm and technical prowess making him an invaluable asset.

The ESS Discovery had been traveling at nearlight speed, its mission to explore distant star systems and seek out new life forms. They had left Earth with high hopes and a sense of adventure, but the journey had taken far longer than any of them had anticipated. Due to the effects of time dilation, what had been a few years for them had been a millennium on Earth.

As they approached their home planet, the crew gathered in the observation deck, eager to see Earth once more. The familiar blue orb hung in the blackness of space, a beacon of life and homecoming.

"Home sweet home," Aria said, a smile spreading across her face. "I've missed that sight."

"Me too," Steven agreed, his eyes fixed on the planet. "I can't wait to see my family again."

The ship began its descent, and the crew prepared for re-entry. As they entered Earth's atmosphere, the ship's systems picked up an unusual signal—a distress beacon, faint but persistent.

"What's that?" Alex asked, his fingers flying over the controls.

"It's a distress signal," Aria said, frowning. "But it's ancient. It must have been active for a long time."

"Let's investigate," Finn suggested. "We need to know what's going on."

As the ship touched down, the astronauts were filled with anticipation. But when the hatch opened and they stepped onto the surface, they were met with a sight that filled them with dread. The landscape was desolate, overgrown with twisted vegetation and crumbling ruins of oncegreat cities.

The air was thick with the stench of decay.

"What happened here?" Eve whispered, her voice trembling.

The crew moved cautiously, their senses on high alert. As they explored the ruins, they found signs of a civilization that had fallen into chaos and ruin. Buildings lay in shambles, vehicles were rusted and abandoned, and everywhere there were signs of a violent struggle.

Then they saw them—the inhabitants of this shattered world. The people, if they could still be called that, were little more than rotting husks, their bodies decaying but still moving, driven by a relentless hunger. Their eyes were vacant, their movements jerky and uncoordinated. These were not the humans the astronauts remembered, but something far more horrifying.

"They're... zombies," Steven said, his voice barely a whisper. "How is this possible?"

Eve knelt beside one of the creatures, her biologist instincts taking over. "It's like their bodies are decomposing, but they're still alive. Something must have caused this."

As they continued to explore, they pieced together the story of what had happened. They found records and data logs, old news broadcasts that told of a mysterious substance from a meteorite that had infected the entire population. The infection spread rapidly, turning people into immortal, decaying creatures driven by an insatiable hunger.

"This must be the result of that substance," Eliot said, examining a dusty terminal. "It turned everyone into these... things."

"But why didn't they die?" Alex asked, horrified. "Why are they still moving?"

"It seems the substance granted a form of immortality," Eve speculated. "But at a terrible cost. Their bodies are rotting, but they can't die."

Aria took a deep breath, trying to process the enormity of their situation. "We need to find out if there's any hope of reversing this. There must be some records, some research that can help us."

The astronauts made their way to what had once been a major research facility. Inside, they found a trove of information—scientific data, research notes, and video logs. It was here that they learned of the original group that had discovered the meteorite and the subsequent spread of the infection.

"We have to find a way to help," Aria said, determination hardening her voice. "We can't let this be the end of humanity."

For days, they pored over the research, trying to understand the substance and its effects. They discovered that the substance had not only affected humans but had spread to every living creature on the planet. Animals, too, were now grotesque, decaying versions of their former selves, driven by the same insatiable hunger.

As they delved deeper into the research, they realized the enormity of the task before them. The infection had spread so thoroughly, so completely, that finding a cure seemed almost impossible. But the astronauts were nothing if not resilient. They had faced the unknown before, and they would do it again.

"We need to gather samples," Eve said, her mind already working on possible solutions. "If we can understand the substance at a molecular level, maybe we can find a way to counteract it."

The crew set out on their mission, collecting samples from the infected, from the environment, and from the ruins of the old world. They worked tirelessly, driven by the hope that they could still save what was left of humanity.

As they continued their research, they discovered a glimmer of hope. In the deepest, most secure labs, they found records of a potential antidote—a substance that could neutralize the infection. It had been in the early stages of development when the world fell apart.

"This is it," Aria said, her voice filled with

determination. "This is our chance to make things right."

The astronauts set to work, using their advanced technology and the knowledge they had gathered. It was a race against time, a desperate bid to save a world that had been lost for a thousand years.

As they worked, they couldn't help but wonder about the people who had come before them. Mike, Jenny, Sam, and Leah—had they survived? Had they continued to search for a cure, even as the world crumbled around them? The astronauts hoped that, wherever they were, those who had set this chain of events in motion would find some solace in knowing that their efforts had not been in vain.

The future of humanity now rested in the hands of these six astronauts, their determination and resilience a beacon of hope in a world overrun by darkness. They knew the road ahead would be long and fraught with challenges, but they were ready. Together, they would fight to reclaim their world, to restore life to a planet lost to the ravages of an alien substance.

And so, under the watchful eyes of the decaying remnants of humanity, the astronauts embarked on their mission to heal the world. They were a symbol of hope, a reminder that even in the darkest of times, the spirit of exploration, discovery, and resilience could still shine through.

Chapter 5
Survival

The Earth the astronauts returned to be a far cry from the one they had left behind. The air was heavy with the stench of decay, and the landscape was a twisted caricature of its former self. Overgrown vegetation choked the ruins of cities, and the groans of the undead echoed through the empty streets. Survival on this ravaged planet would be their greatest challenge yet.

Aria, Steven, Finn, Eve, Eliot, and Alex quickly realized that the food and water supplies aboard the ESS Discovery would only last them about a month. They had to act fast to secure their immediate needs while planning for long-term survival.

Their first priority was to find a defensible location to set up a base. After scouting the area around their landing site, they settled on an abandoned military bunker. It was sturdy, with thick walls and a heavy, reinforced door that could keep the zombies at bay.

"Perfect," Finn said, inspecting the structure. "This place was built to withstand a lot. It'll do for now."

They cleared the bunker of debris and secured the entrances. Finn and Steven worked on setting up solar panels from the ship to provide a reliable power source. Alex rigged up communication equipment, hoping to pick up any signals from other survivors, though the airwaves remained eerily silent.

With their base established, the astronauts turned their attention to scavenging for food and water. They ventured into the nearby ruins, searching abandoned stores, homes, and vehicles. The constant threat of zombies made every outing perilous.

"Stay close and keep quiet," Aria instructed as they moved through the streets. "We don't want to attract any attention."

They found canned goods, bottled water, and other non-perishable items, though much had already been looted or spoiled. Eve, using her knowledge as a biologist, identified plants that were safe to eat and set up a small hydroponic garden inside the bunker.

The zombies were a constant threat. The undead were drawn to any noise or movement, and the astronauts had to be vigilant at all times. They fortified the bunker with makeshift barricades and set up traps around the perimeter.

Eliot, with his medical background, took on the task of treating any injuries and ensuring that everyone stayed healthy. "We can't afford to get
careless," he reminded the team. "One bite, and it's over."

Finn, with his engineering skills, devised weapons and tools from the salvaged materials they found. He created spears, reinforced their makeshift barricades, and even managed to rig a rudimentary alarm system that would alert them to any breaches.

Life settled into a harsh but necessary routine. During the day, they scavenged and worked on fortifying their base. At night, they took turns keeping watch, ensuring that no zombies could sneak up on them while they slept.

Eve continued her research into the infection, using the limited equipment they had salvaged.

She was determined to find a way to reverse the effects of the meteorite substance, but the progress was slow and challenging without the advanced facilities she was used to.

"We need more equipment," Eve said one evening, frustration evident in her voice. "If we could find a laboratory that hasn't been completely ransacked, it would help."

"Let's keep looking," Aria said. "We can't give up hope now."

One particularly harrowing night, the alarm system went off. A horde of zombies had been attracted to their base, possibly by the sound of their scavenging during the day. The team sprang into action, defending their makeshift home with everything they had.

"Here they come!" Alex shouted, grabbing a spear.

The battle was fierce. The zombies were relentless, and the astronauts had to rely on their training and teamwork to fend them off. Steven and Finn used their makeshift weapons to keep the undead at bay, while Aria and Alex took turns securing the doors and reinforcing weak points in their defenses. Eliot and Eve provided support, treating any injuries and ensuring that everyone had what they needed to keep fighting.

"Keep pushing them back!" Aria yelled, swinging a heavy metal pipe at an advancing zombie.

"I'm on it!" Steven responded, thrusting his spear into the chest of another undead, its body collapsing to the ground with a sickening thud.

Eliot quickly wrapped a bandage around Alex's arm where a piece of debris had scratched him. "You're good," he said, giving Alex a reassuring pat on the back.

After what felt like an eternity, the horde began to thin out. The last of the zombies were dispatched, and the team slumped to the ground, exhausted but alive.

"We made it," Steven panted, wiping sweat and grime from his forehead. "Barely."

Despite the constant danger and the harsh realities of their new world, the astronauts remained determined. They were driven by the hope that they could find a way to reverse the infection and restore humanity. Each day was a struggle for survival, but they faced it together, drawing strength from their shared mission and their bond as a team.

Aria stood on the roof of their bunker, looking out over the desolate landscape. The sun was rising, casting a pale light over the ruins. She took a deep breath, feeling the weight of their task but also the resolve to see it through.

"We're not giving up," she said to herself, her voice firm. "We will find a way to fix this."

The astronauts knew that their journey was far from over. They had survived their first month on this ravaged Earth, but the fight was just beginning. Together, they would face whatever came next, driven by the hope of a brighter future and the belief that they could still make a difference.

"Let's keep moving," Aria said to her team as they gathered around her. "We've got work to do."

Finn nodded, determination in his eyes. "We'll make it. One step at a time."

Eve glanced at the makeshift garden she had started. "Every little bit helps. We'll find a way."

Steven clapped Alex on the shoulder. "We stick together, we survive."

Eliot, ever the optimist, smiled. "And who knows, maybe we'll even thrive."

Aria looked at each of them, pride swelling in her chest. "Alright, team. Let's get to work. Our future depends on it."

The astronauts dispersed, each returning to their tasks, their spirits lifted by their shared resolve. They had come a long way, and they were prepared to go even further. In this shattered world, they were a beacon of hope, a reminder that even in the darkest of times, the spirit of exploration, discovery, and resilience could still shine through.

Chapter 6
The Breaking Point

Days turned into weeks, and weeks into months as the astronauts continued their struggle for survival on the ravaged Earth. They scavenged for food and water, fortified their base, and fought off the relentless hordes of zombies that constantly threatened their lives. The routine became their new normal, a grueling existence that tested their endurance and sanity.

Aria kept the team focused and motivated, reminding them daily of their mission to find a cure and restore humanity. Steven and Finn worked tirelessly to improve their defenses and scavenge for supplies, while Eve and Eliot concentrated on their research and tending to their small hydroponic garden. Alex, the youngest and most enthusiastic of the group, took on various tasks, using his technical skills to maintain their communication equipment and assist with any mechanical issues.

But as time passed, the weight of their situation began to take its toll, especially on Alex. The once bright and eager young man started to show signs of strain. He became quieter, his once boundless energy waning. The isolation, the constant danger, and the sheer horror of their reality began to gnaw at his mind.

"Hey, Alex, how's the comms system holding up?" Steven asked one afternoon as they sat together during a rare moment of rest.

Alex shrugged, his eyes distant. "It's fine, I guess. Still no signals, though. It's like we're the only ones left."

"We'll keep trying," Steven said, trying to sound hopeful. "We can't give up."

But Alex's despondency only deepened. He spent more time alone, tinkering with the equipment or staring off into the distance. The others noticed but were too preoccupied with their own struggles to fully grasp the extent of his decline.

One evening, as the team gathered for their meager dinner, Alex sat apart from the group, picking at his food. Aria watched him with concern, her instincts as a leader telling her that something was very wrong.

"Alex, you doing okay?" she asked gently, trying to engage him.

He looked up, his eyes hollow. "Yeah, just tired. It's been a long day."

Eve, sitting beside him, placed a hand on his arm. "We're all tired, Alex. But we're in this together. If you need to talk, we're here for you."

He forced a smile, but it didn't reach his eyes. "Thanks, Eve. I'm fine, really."

The days dragged on, each one blending into the next. The monotony of their survival routine, combined with the constant threat of zombies, created a tense and oppressive atmosphere. It became harder to find moments of respite, and the strain on the group dynamic grew

One night, as the team prepared for bed, Alex seemed particularly agitated. He paced the bunker, his movements erratic.

"Alex, why don't you sit down?" Finn suggested, concern etched on his face. "You need to rest."

"I can't," Alex muttered, running a hand through his hair. "I can't do this anymore. It's too much."

Aria approached him, her expression serious. "Alex, we need to stay strong. We're all feeling it, but we have to keep going."

He turned to her, desperation in his eyes. "What if we never find a cure? What if we're stuck like this forever?"

"We can't think that way," Aria replied firmly. "We have to believe we can make a difference."

But Alex couldn't be consoled. He retreated to a corner of the bunker, his mind racing with dark thoughts. As the others settled into their sleeping bags, uneasy but exhausted, Alex sat alone, his despair deepening.

Hours passed, and the bunker was silent save for the occasional groan of a distant zombie. Suddenly, a loud bang shattered the stillness, jerking everyone awake.

"What was that?" Steven exclaimed, scrambling to his feet.

They rushed to where the sound had come from, their hearts pounding with fear. In the dim light, they found Alex slumped against the wall, blood pooling around him. The gun lay at his side, the reality of what had happened hitting them all at once.

"No!" Aria screamed, dropping to her knees beside him. "Alex, no!"

Eliot pushed through the group, his medical training taking over. He checked for a pulse, but it was clear there was nothing he could do. Tears filled his eyes as he shook his head. "He's gone."

The team was stunned, their minds struggling to process the loss. Eve sobbed quietly, while Finn and Steven stood in shock, unable to speak.

Aria's hands trembled as she gently closed Alex's eyes. "Why didn't we see this coming?" she whispered, her voice breaking. "Why didn't we help him?"

"We were all so focused on surviving," Finn said, his voice choked with emotion. "We didn't see how much he was hurting."

"We failed him," Eve said, tears streaming down her face. "We should have done more."

Eliot placed a hand on Aria's shoulder. "We need to honor him by continuing our mission. We can't let his death be in vain."

The loss of Alex was a devastating blow, a stark reminder of the mental and emotional toll their situation had taken on them all. They decided to bury him in the middle of their base, in a place where they could always remember him and draw strength from his memory. They dug a grave inside the bunker, marking it with a simple cross made from scavenged wood. It was a somber ceremony, each of them saying their goodbyes in their own way.

As they stood around his grave, Aria spoke, her voice filled with grief and determination. "We have to keep going. For Alex, for ourselves, for humanity. We can't let this be the end."

The team nodded, their resolve hardening in the face of their loss. They returned to their tasks, their hearts heavy but their determination renewed. They knew that the road ahead would be even more challenging, but they were committed to seeing it through.

Alex's death had shown them the fragility of their hope and the importance of supporting each other. They vowed to be more vigilant, more attentive to each other's needs, and more united in their fight for survival.

The days that followed were difficult, the memory of Alex's struggle and death a constant shadow over their efforts. But the astronauts pressed on, driven by the promise they had made to him and to themselves. They continued to scavenger, to defend their base, and to work towards finding a cure, their bond as a team stronger than ever.

In the end, it was their shared hope and determination that kept them going. They knew that as long as they had each other, they had a chance. And they were determined to make that chance count, no matter what it took.

Chapter 7
Flowers and Shadows

The days following Alex's tragic death were shrouded in a somber haze. The astronauts continued their routine, but the loss had left a gaping hole in their hearts. Each of them struggled with the weight of grief, but they also knew that they had to keep moving forward.

One morning, Aria gathered the team together. "We need to do something for Alex," she said softly. "Something to honor his memory."

Eve nodded, her eyes red from crying. "I agree. We should find something beautiful in this wasteland, something that reminds us of who he was."

Steven and Finn exchanged glances, then Steven spoke up. "There are a few patches of wildflowers we've seen while scavenging. They're rare, but they're out there. We could gather some for his grave."

With a renewed sense of purpose, the team set out to find the flowers. It was a difficult task; the barren landscape was mostly devoid of life, and the ever-present danger of zombies made every excursion perilous. Still, they pressed on, driven by their desire to do something meaningful for their fallen friend.

After hours of searching, they finally stumbled upon a small patch of wildflowers nestled in the shadow of a crumbling building. The flowers were hardy and resilient, a splash of color in an otherwise gray world.

"These are perfect," Eve said, her voice tinged with both sadness and relief. She carefully picked a handful of the flowers, the delicate petals a stark contrast to the harsh reality around them.

They returned to the base with their precious find, and together they arranged the flowers on Alex's grave. The simple cross stood in the center of the bunker, a silent testament to their loss. The flowers added a touch of beauty and hope, a reminder of the life they were fighting to reclaim.

Aria knelt beside the grave, her fingers brushing against the petals. "Alex, we miss you," she whispered. "But we're going to keep fighting. We're going to find a way to make this right."

The team stood in silence for a moment, each of them lost in their own thoughts. The flowers swayed gently in the air, a poignant reminder of the fragility of life.

Suddenly, Steven's sharp intake of breath broke the silence. He was staring out one of the narrow windows of the bunker. "Zombies," he said, his voice tense. "A lot of them, heading this way."

Aria stood up, her expression hardening.
"Everyone, get ready. We knew this could happen. We need to protect ourselves and our base."

Finn and Steven quickly checked their weapons, making sure they were loaded and ready. Eve and Eliot gathered their makeshift defenses, while Aria took a deep breath, steeling herself for the fight ahead.

The sound of the approaching horde grew louder, the groans and shuffling footsteps creating an ominous chorus. The team moved into position, their faces set with determination.

"We can do this," Aria said, her voice steady. "Remember what we're fighting for. For Alex, for ourselves, and for the future."

The first zombies appeared on the horizon, their decaying bodies moving with a relentless, mindless hunger. The astronauts braced themselves, their hearts pounding in their chests.

As the zombies drew closer, Aria raised her weapon. "Aim for the head," she reminded them. "It's the only way to take them down for good."

The battle was fierce and chaotic. The astronauts fought with everything they had, their movements precise and focused. Steven and Finn took down zombies with well-placed shots, while Eve and Eliot used their makeshift defenses to keep the creatures at bay. Aria moved among them, providing support and encouragement, her leadership keeping them focused and coordinated.

Despite the overwhelming numbers, the team held their ground. They fought with a determination born of desperation and hope, their bond as a team giving them strength. The memory of Alex's sacrifice drove them on, fueling their resolve.

Finally, after what felt like an eternity, the last of the zombies fell. The team stood among the carnage, their bodies exhausted but their spirits unbroken.

Aria lowered her weapon, her breathing heavy. "We did it," she said, her voice filled with a mix of relief and sorrow. "We survived."

Eve collapsed to her knees, tears streaming down her face. "For Alex," she whispered. "We did this for Alex."

The others gathered around her, their faces reflecting the same mixture of emotions. They had faced unimaginable horrors and had come through it together, stronger and more determined than ever.

Aria looked at the flowers on Alex's grave, their vibrant colors a stark contrast to the grim reality of their world. "We'll keep fighting," she said softly. "We'll keep surviving. For Alex, and for all of us."

The team nodded, their resolve renewed. They knew that the road ahead would be filled with challenges, but they were ready to face them together. United by their shared loss and their unwavering hope, they would continue their fight for survival and for a better future.

Chapter 8
Bonds of Survival

The loss of their friend had a profound impact on the group, but it also brought them closer together, especially Eve and Finn. Their bond, always strong, became the bedrock on which they leaned in their darkest moments.

Eve and Finn had known each other long before the world descended into chaos. Their friendship had been a cornerstone of their lives, providing a sense of stability and comfort. But in this new, harsh reality, their relationship had deepened into something more complex and profound.

One evening, as the sun dipped below the horizon, casting a warm glow over their battered base, Eve and Finn found themselves working together to repair a section of the perimeter fence. The task was slow and continues, but it gave them time to be alone, away from the pressures and prying eyes of the others.

“Pass me the wrench,” Finn said, his voice low and steady.

Eve handed it over, their fingers brushing lightly. She hesitated, then spoke, her voice tinged with a mix of nostalgia and sadness. “Do you ever think about... before? Before all this happened?”

Finn paused, looking at her with eyes that reflected the same weariness she felt. “Yeah, I do. All the time. It feels like a different world.”

Eve nodded, her throat tight. "Sometimes I wonder what we would be doing now if things were different. If we were still back then."

Finn set down the wrench and turned to face her fully. "I think about that too. But we can't change what happened. We can only move forward, together."

Their eyes locked, and for a moment, the weight of their losses and the horrors they had faced seemed to melt away. In that quiet, intimate moment, they found solace in each other's presence. It was a connection that went beyond words, a deep, unspoken understanding.

As they resumed their work, the silence between them was no longer empty but filled with unspoken feelings and shared memories. They finished the repairs as the last light faded, then sat down to rest, their shoulders brushing.

“Remember that day we stayed up all night talking about our dreams?” Eve asked, her voice soft.

Finn smiled, a rare, genuine smile. “I remember, you wanted to travel the world. I wanted to build a home. Funny how things turn out.”

Eve’s heart ached with the memory, but she smiled too. “Yeah. But in a way, we’re still building something. We’re building a future, even if it’s not the one we imagined.”

Finn reached out and took her hand, his touch warm and reassuring. “As long as we’re together, we’ll figure it out. One step at a time.”

Eve squeezed his hand, her eyes shining with unshed tears. “I don’t know what I’d do without you, Finn. You’re my anchor.”

“And you’re mine,” Finn replied, his voice steady. “We’ll get through this, together.”

In the days that followed, their bond only grew stronger. They shared quiet moments, stolen glances, and whispered conversations that kept their spirits alive. Each day was a battle, but knowing they had each other made it bearable.

One night, as they sat by the fire, Finn looked at Eve with a seriousness that made her heart skip a beat. "Eve, I know we don't talk about it much, but... I need you to know how much you mean to me. You're the reason I keep fighting."

Eve felt a lump in her throat, but she met his gaze with unwavering determination. "I feel the same way, Finn. We've lost so much, but we still have each other. And that means everything to me."

They leaned in, their foreheads touching, drawing strength from each other. In a world filled with death and despair, their love was a beacon of hope, a reminder of what they were fighting for.

As they faced each new challenge, their bond remained unbreakable. They fought for their survival, not just for themselves but for each other. In the end, it was their love that gave them the strength to keep going, to face the unknown with courage and determination.

Eve and Finn's story was one of resilience and hope, a testament to the power of love in even the darkest of times. And as long as they had each other, they knew they could face whatever came next, hand in hand, heart to heart.

Chapter 9
Sacrifice

The days following their solemn tribute to Alex were marked by an uneasy calm. The team fell into a rhythm, their daily routines bringing a semblance of normalcy to their chaotic world. But in the back of their minds, they knew that danger was never far away.

One evening, as they were fortifying the bunker's perimeter, Steven noticed something on the horizon. A dark mass, moving steadily towards them.

“Guys, we’ve got a situation,” he called out, his voice laced with urgency.

Aria, Finn, Eve, and Eliot rushed to his side, peering into the distance. The sight made their blood run cold—a massive swarm of zombies, far larger than any they had encountered before, was advancing towards their base.

“We need to prepare for a fight,” Aria said, her voice steady but her heart pounding. “Eliot, get the weapons. Steven, Finn, let’s reinforce the barricades. Eve, help me set up the traps.”

The team moved with practiced efficiency, each member focused on their task. The impending battle loomed over them like a dark cloud, but they were determined to protect their base and each other.

As the swarm drew closer, the tension in the air became palpable. The groans of the zombies grew louder, a haunting symphony of death.

“They’re almost here!” Steven shouted. “Get ready!”

The first wave hit with brutal force. Zombies clawed and snarled at the barricades, their decaying bodies pressing against the defenses. The team fought back with everything they had, firing their weapons and using makeshift melee tools to fend off the attackers.

Eve and Eliot worked in tandem, their movements synchronized as they struck down zombie after zombie. Finn and Steven held the front line, their weapons blazing. Aria moved between them, her leadership and combat skills keeping the team coordinated.

But the swarm was relentless, and soon the barricades began to give way. The team was forced to fall back, retreating towards the inner sanctum of their base.

“Keep moving! Don’t let them surround us!” Aria shouted, her voice cutting through the chaos.

Despite their efforts, the sheer number of zombies began to overwhelm them. In the confusion, Eve found herself separated from the others. She turned, only to realize she was trapped in a tightening circle of undead.

“Help!” she screamed, her voice tinged with desperation

Finn’s heart leaped into his throat when he saw her predicament. Without a second thought, he charged towards her, plowing through the zombies with a ferocity fueled by fear and love.

"Eve, get down!" he yelled as he reached her, swinging his weapon with deadly precision.

Eve dropped to the ground just as Finn unleashed a flurry of blows, clearing a path through the zombies. He grabbed her hand, pulling her to her feet.

"Come on, we've got to move!" he urged.

They fought their way back towards the others, but the zombies closed in faster than they could escape. In a moment of horrifying clarity, Finn realized what he had to do.

"Go, Eve! Get to the others!" he shouted, pushing her forward.

Eve's eyes widened in terror. "No, I'm not leaving you!"

"You have to!" Finn insisted, his voice breaking. "Go!"

Tears streaming down her face, Eve hesitated, but the urgency in Finn's eyes forced her to comply. She turned and ran, her heart shattering with every step.

Finn turned back to face the zombies, his weapon raised. He fought with everything he had, buying Eve the precious seconds she needed to reach safety. But the swarm was too much, and soon he was overwhelmed.

From a distance, Aria, Steven, and Eliot saw what was happening. "Finn!" Steven shouted, but it was too late. They watched in helpless horror as Finn was consumed by the horde.

Eve reached the others, her face a mask of anguish. "He's gone," she whispered, collapsing into Aria's arms.

The team regrouped, their grief fuelling their determination. With renewed vigour, they fought off the remaining zombies, finally driving the last of them away. The base was in ruins, but they were alive.

As the dust settled, the reality of their loss hit them hard. They gathered around the spot where Finn had made his last stand, the weight of his sacrifice heavy on their hearts.

"He saved my life," Eve said through her tears. "He saved all of us."

Aria placed a hand on Eve's shoulder, her own eyes glistening with tears. "He was a hero. We owe it to him to keep going."

Steven and Eliot nodded, their expressions grim but resolute. They knew that Finn's sacrifice could not be in vain.

The team worked together to repair the base, their movements slower and more deliberate as they processed their grief. They buried Finn beside Alex, marking his grave with A big rock that had his name engraved in the centre. Eve placed the last of the wildflowers they had gathered on his grave, her hands trembling.

As they stood around the grave, Aria spoke, her voice steady despite the sorrow that filled it. “We’ve lost so much, but we still have each other. We’ll keep fighting, for Alex, for Finn, and for ourselves.”

The team nodded, drawing strength from each other. The fight was far from over, but they were determined to honour the memory of their fallen friends by continuing to survive and seek a way to save humanity.

In the fading light of the day, they stood together, a united front against the darkness that threatened to consume them. They were more than a team; they were a family, bound by their shared struggles and the sacrifices of those they had lost.

And as long as they had each other, they would keep fighting, no matter what.

Chapter 10
The Weight of Grief

The loss of Finn casts a long shadow over the group. Each member struggled with their grief in their own way, but none more so than Eve. The bond she had shared with Finn was deeper than any other, and his absence left a void that seemed impossible to fill.

Days turned into weeks, and the group tried to maintain their routine, clinging to the semblance of normalcy they had built in their crumbling world. But the pain of their losses lingered, a constant reminder of the friends they had buried.

Eve's grief was a palpable force. She spent hours sitting by Finn's grave, her eyes hollow and vacant. The others watched her with growing concern, unsure of how to help her through the depths of her sorrow.

"Eve, you need to eat something," Aria said gently one morning, placing a small portion of their meager rations in front of her.

Eve shook her head, her voice barely a whisper. "I'm not hungry."

Aria exchanged worried glances with Steven and Eliot. "Eve, please. You have to keep your strength up. Finn wouldn't want you to—"

"Don't," Eve interrupted, her voice cracking.
"Don't tell me what Finn would want. He's gone, Aria. He's gone because of me."

Steven knelt beside her, his expression pained. "Eve, it wasn't your fault. He made his choice to save you. He cared about you.

Tears welled in Eve's eyes, but she remained silent, her gaze fixed on the ground. The others tried to console her, offering words of comfort and support, but nothing seemed to reach her.

Days passed, and Eve's condition worsened. She grew weaker, her frame becoming gaunt and frail. The team watched helplessly as she withered away, her spirit seemingly crushed under the weight of her grief.

One night, as they gathered around the fire, Eliot tried to lighten the mood with one of his jokes. "You know, if Finn were here, he'd probably be complaining about how bad my cooking is.

The attempt at humor fell flat, and the silence that followed was heavy with sadness. Eve didn't even react, her eyes distant and unfocused.

Aria couldn't bear it any longer. She knelt beside Eve, taking her cold, trembling hands in her own. "Eve, please. We can't lose you too. We need you."

Eve's eyes met Aria's, a flicker of life returning for a brief moment. "I... I miss him so much," she whispered, her voice broken.

"We all do," Aria said softly, tears streaming down her face. "But we have to keep going. For Finn. For Alex. For all of us."

Eve closed her eyes, a single tear slipping down her cheek. "I'm sorry, Aria. I just... I can't."

The next morning, they found Eve lying still beside Finn's grave, her body emaciated and lifeless. The reality of her loss hit them like a physical blow, their hearts breaking all over again.

Steven's voice was choked with emotion as he knelt beside her. "She didn't deserve this. None of us do."

Eliot, usually so full of jokes and laughter, was uncharacteristically silent. He helped Aria and Steven dig a grave beside Finn's, their movements slow and deliberate as they worked through their grief.

They laid Eve to rest beside Finn, marking her grave with a simple cross made from scavenged wood. Aria placed the last of the flowers they had found on her grave, her heart heavy with sorrow.

As they stood around the grave, the weight of their losses seemed almost too much to bear. The team had been whittled down, their numbers and their hope diminished. But they knew they had to keep moving forward, if only to honor the memory of those they had lost.

Aria spoke, her voice steady despite the tears that threatened to fall. "We’ve lost so much, but we have to keep going. For Eve, for Finn, for Alex. We owe it to them to survive."

Steven and Eliot nodded, their faces grim but resolute. They knew the road ahead would be filled with challenges, but they were determined to face them together.

In the dim light of the bunker, they drew strength from each other, their bonds of friendship and shared grief keeping them from falling into despair. They had lost so much, but they still had each other, and that was enough to keep fighting.

As the sun set, casting long shadows over the barren landscape, the team gathered around the fire. They sat in silence, the weight of their grief a constant presence, but their determination unbroken. They would continue to survive, to honor the memory of their fallen friends, and to fight for a future where their sacrifices would not be in vain.

In the end, they were more than survivors; they were a family, bound together by love, loss, and the unyielding spirit of humanity. And as long as they had each other, they would keep fighting, no matter what.

Chapter 11
The Last Stand

The days following Eve's death were marked by a heavy silence, each of the survivors grappling with their grief and the relentless threat of the zombie hordes. Supplies were running low, and the oncedefendable base felt increasingly fragile. The group knew it was only a matter of time before they would face another attack.

One evening, as the sun dipped below the horizon, casting long shadows over their fortified base, Steven, Eliot, and Aria gathered around the perimeter. Steven's sharp eyes caught movement in the distance.

"They're coming," he said, his voice tense. "And it looks like there's more of them this time."

Aria, her face set with determination, nodded. "Everyone, get ready. We need to hold them off as long as we can."

The swarm moved with a terrifying speed and coordination, their grotesque forms silhouetted against the twilight. These zombies were different—faster, stronger, more relentless. The group braced for the onslaught, each member taking their position, weapons ready.

As the first wave hit, the air filled with the sounds of gunfire and snarling undead. The group fought with everything they had, their desperation lending them a fierce strength. Aria, her eyes blazing with a mix of anger and determination, took the lead, her rifle spitting bullets with deadly precision.

"They're too strong!" Eliot shouted, his voice barely audible over the chaos. "We need to fall back!"

But Aria was in the zone, her focus entirely on the zombies in front of her. She advanced steadily, each shot clearing a path through the horde. Steven and Eliot shouted after her, their voices filled with panic.

"Aria, get back!" Steven yelled. "You're going too far!"

"Aria, please!" Eliot added, desperation in his voice.

But Aria didn't listen. She moved forward, her every step deliberate, until she reached a small outpost a short distance from their main base. The structure was rickety but provided a vantage point. She climbed to the top, taking the high ground

From her elevated position, Aria picked off zombies with an almost mechanical efficiency. The rest of the group watched in a mixture of awe and fear, knowing that she was putting herself in extreme danger.

"She's too far out," Steven muttered, his hands trembling as he reloaded his weapon. "We can't cover her from here."

Eliot's face was pale, his eyes wide with fear. "We have to get her back. She's going to get herself killed."

But before they could formulate a plan, the unthinkable happened. A zombie managed to breach the base of the outpost, its weight causing the fragile structure to shudder. Aria, caught off guard, lost her footing. Time seemed to slow as she fell from the tower, hitting the ground with a sickening thud.

"Aria!" Steven and Eliot screamed in unison; their voices raw with horror.

The zombies swarmed over her, their grotesque forms obscuring her from view. Steven and Eliot fought their way towards her, their hearts pounding with a mix of fear and rage. But by the time they reached her, it was too late.

Aria's lifeless body lay on the ground, the zombies already moving on to new prey. Steven and Eliot stood over her, their breaths coming in ragged gasps, their minds struggling to process the loss.

"She's gone," Steven whispered, his voice choked with emotion. "She's really gone."

Eliot fell to his knees beside her, tears streaming down his face. "Why didn't she listen? Why didn't she come back?"

Steven placed a hand on Eliot's shoulder, his own eyes glistening with tears. "She was trying to protect us. She always put us first."

The two men were overcome with a torrent of emotions—grief, anger, guilt. They had lost their leader, their friend, the person who had held them together through so many trials.

As the last of the zombies were driven away, Steven and Eliot carried Aria's body back to the base. The once-strong fortress felt emptier than ever, the weight of their losses pressing down on them with an almost unbearable force.

They buried Aria beside Alex, Finn, and Eve, their hearts heavy with sorrow. The grave markers stood as silent sentinels, a testament to the sacrifices made and the lives lost.

In the quiet aftermath, Steven and Eliot sat by the graves, the enormity of their situation settling over them. They were the last of their group, their family, and the burden of survival felt heavier than ever.

"We have to keep going," Steven said quietly, his voice filled with a steely resolve. "For Aria. For all of them.

Eliot nodded, wiping the tears from his eyes. "We will. We'll keep fighting. We'll survive."

As the sun rose on another day in their ravaged world, the two survivors stood together, their bond forged in the crucible of loss and determination. They had lost so much, but they still had each other. And as long as they had that, they would continue to fight, no matter what.

Chapter 12
The Final Front

The days blurred together as Steven and Eliot continued their relentless battle against the zombies. The once-overwhelming swarms had begun to dwindle, and there were moments when they dared to hope that perhaps the worst was behind them. But the memory of their fallen friends kept them vigilant, knowing that complacency could be deadly.

One morning, as the sun cast a pale light over their battered base, Steven and Eliot prepared for another day of survival. They fortified their defenses and rationed their remaining supplies, their movements driven by the muscle memory of routine.

“Think this could be the last of them?” Eliot asked, his tone hopeful yet weary.

Steven shrugged, his eyes scanning the horizon. “I don’t know. But we have to stay ready. We can’t let our guard down.”

As they patrolled the perimeter, the familiar sound of shuffling feet and guttural moans reached their ears. A small group of zombies had appeared, and the two men moved into position, their weapons at the ready.

“Here we go again,” Eliot muttered, raising his rifle.

The fight was swift and brutal, their years of practice making quick work of the undead. As the last zombie fell, Steven and Eliot exchanged a glance, a silent acknowledgment of their efficiency.

But before they could catch their breath, a distant rumble caught their attention. The ground seemed to vibrate beneath their feet, and a dark mass appeared on the horizon, moving with a horrifying speed.

“Steven... look,” Eliot said, his voice trembling.

Steven’s eyes widened in horror as he realized what was coming. A horde of zombies—two hundred strong—was rushing towards their base, an unstoppable wave of death.

“Get ready!” Steven shouted, his voice cracking with urgency. “We have to hold them off!”

Eliot moved to the front of the base, his rifle raised, while Steven circled around to cover the flanks. The horde descended upon them with terrifying speed, their numbers overwhelming the makeshift defenses.

Eliot fired rapidly, each shot finding its mark, but the sheer volume of zombies made it impossible to hold them back. “There’s too many of them!” he shouted, panic creeping into his voice.

“Keep fighting!” Steven yelled from the other side, his own weapon blazing.

The horde pressed closer, and despite their best efforts, the zombies began to break through. Eliot found himself at the epicenter of the chaos, his heart pounding as the undead surged towards him.

“Steven! I need help!” Eliot screamed, but the noise of the battle drowned out his plea.

A zombie lunged at Eliot, its decayed hands clawing at his face. He fought back desperately, but another zombie grabbed him from behind, and then another. He was surrounded, their rotting bodies pressing in on him.

“No! Get off me!” Eliot shouted, his voice filled with terror. He felt a searing pain as the zombies’ teeth sank into his flesh, their grotesque mouths tearing at his skin.

“Eliot!” Steven’s voice cut through the chaos, filled with horror. He fought his way towards his friend, but it was too late

Eliot’s screams echoed across the base as the zombies overwhelmed him, their ravenous hunger consuming him alive. Blood poured from his wounds, his body convulsing in agony. The sight was unbearable, and Steven’s heart shattered as he watched his friend being devoured.

“Eliot, no!” Steven cried, his voice breaking. He fired wildly at the zombies, his vision blurred by tears.

But the horde was relentless, their numbers too great to overcome.

As the last of Eliot's screams faded, Steven felt a wave of grief and rage wash over him. He fought with a fury born of loss, cutting down zombie after zombie until his ammo ran dry. Grabbing a makeshift weapon, he continued the fight, his mind a storm of pain and anger.

The battle raged on, and as the sun began to set, the last of the zombies finally fell. Steven stood amidst the carnage, his breath coming in ragged gasps, his body shaking with exhaustion and grief.

He stumbled to where Eliot's lifeless body lay, blood pooling around him. Steven fell to his knees, his tears mingling with the dirt and blood. "I'm so sorry, Eliot," he whispered, his voice choked with emotion. "I'm so sorry."

The loss of Eliot felt like a dagger to the heart. Steven was alone now, the last of their group, surrounded by the graves of his friends. The weight of their sacrifices pressed down on him, almost too much to bear.

As the darkness settled over the base, Steven buried Eliot beside Aria, Finn, and Eve. He marked the grave with a simple cross, his hands trembling with sorrow. The once-busy base was now a graveyard, a testament to the resilience and ultimate sacrifice of his friends.

Steven sat by the graves, his heart heavy with grief. He knew he had to keep going, to honor the memory of those he had lost. But for the first time, the weight of his loneliness felt almost too much to bear.

In the quiet of the night, Steven made a silent vow. He would survive, not just for himself, but for Eliot, Aria, Finn, Eve, and Alex. He would carry their memory with him, fighting to the very end, no matter what.

As the first light of dawn broke over the horizon, Steven stood, his resolve hardening. He was the last of their family, and he would keep fighting, for as long as it took, until there was nothing left to fight for.

Chapter 13
The Final Surrender

Steven's days blended into an endless cycle of survival and solitude. The weight of his losses pressed down on him like a physical burden, each moment filled with the echoes of his friends' voices and the haunting memories of their final moments. The base, once a place of camaraderie and hope, now felt like a tomb.

He spent his days scavenging for food and water, his movements mechanical and devoid of purpose. Nights were the worst, the silence broken only by the distant moans of zombies and the occasional rustle of the wind. Steven's thoughts were consumed by the faces of Aria, Eliot, Finn, Eve, and Alex, their smiles and laughter now replaced by the horror of their deaths.

Steven's depression deepened with each passing day. He barely slept, barely ate, and his will to survive dwindled. The loneliness was a constant, gnawing ache, and the memories of his friends became both a comfort and a torment.

One morning, as Steven sat by the graves of his fallen friends, he whispered to them, his voice raw with emotion. "I miss you all so much. I don't know how much longer I can do this."

He spent hours by the graves, talking to his friends as if they could hear him, as if they could somehow respond and ease his suffering. But the silence that followed was always crushing.

One fateful evening, as the sun dipped below the horizon, Steven noticed a familiar rumble in the distance. His heart sank as he recognized the sound—a horde of zombies, larger than any he had faced before, was approaching the base.

He stood and walked to the perimeter, his heart pounding in his chest. The horde moved like a tidal wave, a mass of rotting flesh and relentless hunger. Steven knew that this time, there was no way he could fight them off alone.

For a moment, he considered running, but the thought of continuing this existence, alone and haunted by memories, was unbearable. A sense of resignation washed over him, and he made a decision.

Steven dropped his weapon and began to walk towards the advancing horde. His steps were slow and deliberate, his mind a storm of fear and sorrow. As he moved closer, the zombies' grotesque faces came into focus, their eyes empty and devoid of humanity.

Tears streamed down Steven's face as he approached the horde. He was scared, more scared than he had ever been, but the thought of rejoining his friends, even in death, brought a strange sense of peace.

"I'm sorry," he whispered to the wind, his voice trembling. "I'm sorry I couldn't save you. I'm sorry I couldn't be stronger."

The first zombie reached him, its decayed hands grabbing at his clothes. Steven felt a sharp pain as its teeth sank into his flesh, but he didn't fight back. He allowed the horde to envelop him, their bites and claws tearing at his body.

As the pain intensified, Steven's sobs grew louder. "I'm sorry!" he cried out, his voice breaking. "I'm so sorry!"

The zombies pulled him to the ground, their ravenous hunger consuming him. Steven's vision blurred, and the world around him began to fade. In his final moments, he thought of his friends, their faces smiling and full of life. He held onto those memories as the darkness closed in.

And then, there was nothing.

The horde moved on, leaving behind the remains of the last survivor of a once-hopeful group. The base, now silent and empty, stood as a testament to the bravery, friendship, and sacrifices of those who had fought to the very end.

In the quiet aftermath, the wind whispered through the ruins, carrying with it the echoes of the past. The world had moved on, but the memories of Steven, Aria, Eliot, Finn, Eve, and Alex remained, a haunting reminder of the cost of survival and the enduring strength of human connection, even in the face of unimaginable horror.

The End

www.ingramcontent.com/pod-product-compliance
Lightning Source LLC
La Vergne TN
LVHW040942150826
845672LV00002B/501

* 9 7 9 8 2 3 0 2 8 7 6 8 1 *